How many 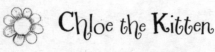 books have you collected?

- 🌼 Chloe the Kitten
- 🌼 Bella the Bunny
- 🌼 Paddy the Puppy
- 🌼 Mia the Mouse
- 🌼 Hailey the Hedgehog
- 🌼 Sophie the Squirrel
- 🌼 Poppy the Pony
- 🌼 Daisy the Deer
- ✓ Betsy the Bunny

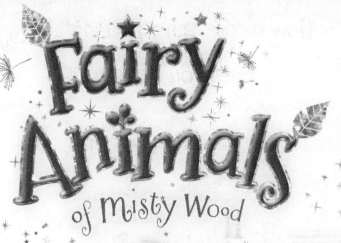

Fairy Animals
of Misty Wood

Betsy the Bunny

Lily Small

EGMONT

With special thanks to Susannah Leigh

EGMONT
We bring stories to life

Betsy the Bunny first published in Great Britain 2014
by Egmont UK Limited
The Yellow Building, 1 Nicholas Road, London W11 4AN

Text copyright © 2014 Hothouse Fiction Ltd
Illustrations copyright © 2014 Artful Doodlers
All rights reserved

ISBN 978 1 4052 6872 1
1 3 5 7 9 10 8 6 4 2

www.egmont.co.uk

www.hothousefiction.com

www.fairyanimals.com

A CIP catalogue record for this title is available from the British Library

Printed and bound in Great Britain by The CPI Group

55767/1

EGMONT LUCKY COIN

Our story began over a century ago, when seventeen-year-old Egmont Harald Petersen found a coin in the street.

He was on his way to buy a flyswatter, a small hand-operated printing machine that he then set up in his tiny apartment.

The coin brought him such good luck that today Egmont has offices in over 30 countries around the world. And that lucky coin is still kept at the company's head offices in Denmark.

Contents

CHAPTER ONE

A Breakfast Surprise

Spring had come to Misty Wood.
The icy frosts of winter had melted
away and the earth was warm and
bouncy again. On the hillsides,
the sweet scent of lavender drifted

gently on the breeze. Soft clover carpeted the valleys and, in the meadows, hundreds of new flowers were just ready to bloom.

Below a cluster of mulberry bushes, in a cosy burrow deep inside the Misty Wood rabbit warren, somebody was bursting with happiness.

'. . . and then I'll twitch my nose and the beautiful buds will unfurl and springtime will have

arrived in Misty Wood at last!'

Betsy the Bud Bunny sat at the old log that was her family's breakfast table, chattering away. She was so excited that her pretty pink wings kept fluttering, and she had to hold on to the table to stop herself from flying off.

Betsy's mum was bustling about the warm burrow. Her dad was busy tweaking his whiskers and arranging his long floppy ears. And her baby brother, Bobby,

was sitting on his toadstool high chair, playing with his mashed carrot. Betsy leaned across the log table and put her little pink nose close to Bobby's face.

'I'll twitch my nose like this, Bobby,' she said, wiggling her nose slowly. 'I have to be careful because the petals are very delicate. If I do it too quickly the flower might break. Ouch!' she yelped as Bobby whacked the tip of her nose with his little white paw.

'Bweak! Bweak!' the baby bunny cried.

Betsy laughed. 'When you're

a bigger Bud Bunny you'll understand.' She fluttered her tiny pink wings proudly. Like all the fairy animals living in Misty Wood, she had a very special job to do to make sure it stayed such a magical place.

A Bud Bunny's special job was to unfurl the flowers and reveal their beautiful blooms. Betsy was a very young Bud Bunny and this was only her second springtime.

Her white cotton tail fluffed up
with happiness as she thought
back to last year. All the other Bud
Bunnies had said she'd done really
well. This year she was determined
to do even better.

And maybe if I'm really good,
Betsy thought, *I might even see the
Easter Bunny at the Misty Wood
Easter Egg Hunt.* Her mum always
said that no one got to meet the
Easter Bunny, because he was so

8

busy and important. But Betsy still hoped that one day, she'd be really lucky.

'I'm sure I'll see all sorts of lovely flowers today,' Betsy said dreamily. 'Big ones and small ones. Pink ones and blue ones. Short ones and tall ones and some in-between ones and . . .'

'Betsy, if you don't stop chattering and finish up your food, it will be time for bed before

you've even started,' her mum said, stirring a wooden pot of fresh elderflower juice.

'Sorry,' Betsy said with a grin. 'I'm just so happy. I've been waiting for today *forever*!'

Her mum set the pot down on the log table. 'Well, you can wait just a little bit longer and have a nice big drink first. It's a lovely sunny day outside and I don't want you getting thirsty.'

She poured some of the sweet juice
into Betsy's acorn cup and the
little bunny gulped it eagerly.

'Yum, that was delicious,' she said, licking her lips. 'Now, I can't hang around. I've got to hurry, hurry, hurry – *hic*!'

Betsy stopped, open-mouthed.

Bobby giggled.

Betsy's mum gasped.

Betsy's dad raised an eyebrow.

Betsy tried again.

'Goodbye, everyone,' she said. 'I'm off to – *hic*!' She stopped and looked around the burrow in

dismay. 'What's –
hic – happening?'
she wailed.

'Oh, Betsy,'
her mum said,
shaking her head. 'You
drank your juice so quickly, it's
given you the hiccups.'

'Hiccups?' Betsy cried. 'But
how am I – *hic* – going to do my
– *hic* – job now? I'll never be able
to keep still enough to unfurl the

13

flower petals if I've got the – *hic* – hiccups!'

And, with that, a fat tear trickled down her snowy white face and landed – splat! – into her empty acorn cup.

CHAPTER TWO
The Cheeky Pollen Puppy

'Cheer up,' Betsy's dad said. He hopped over and patted her on the head with one of his big furry paws. 'Hiccups don't last forever.

15

Once you're flying around outside they'll soon disappear.'

'Really – *hic* – truly?' Betsy said hopefully.

'Really truly,' her dad replied with a smile.

'Dad's right,' Betsy's mum said. 'The fresh air is sure to get rid of your hiccups.'

Betsy glanced at the dandelion clock on the wall.

'Ooh,' she squeaked when she

saw the time blowing away. 'I'd better go. I've got buds to – *hic* – unfurl.'

She said a hasty and hiccuppy goodbye to her family and set off through the Misty Wood rabbit warren. As she scampered along the tunnels, she passed the homes of the other Bud Bunnies. Many of them were getting ready to go out and unfurl the flowers too, so there was lots of hustle and bustle.

'Isn't it exciting, Betsy? Springtime at last!' a little grey bunny called out, twitching his floppy ears. It was Ben, one of Betsy's best friends.

'Hello, Ben!' Betsy said with a smile. 'Yes, it's really exciting – *hic*. Oh, no, not again!' Betsy covered her mouth with her paw.

'Oh, Betsy,' Ben said, looking worried. 'Was that a hiccup?'

'Yes.' Betsy sighed. 'Of all the

mornings to get them, why did it
have to be this one?'

'That *is* bad luck.' Ben tipped
his head to one side thoughtfully.

'But I'm sure they'll disappear when you get outside. Mum says fresh air and sunshine cure everything.'

'I hope she's right,' Betsy said. 'See you up there then, Ben – *hic*!'

Ben grinned at her and waved goodbye.

Betsy turned the corner and saw a bright yellow glow at the end of the tunnel ahead of her. She scampered towards it and

emerged, blinking, into the golden
spring sunshine of Misty Wood.
As her eyes grew used to the light,
she gasped in delight. Spread
out before her was Honeydew
Meadow. Its bright green grass
was carpeted with new flowers, all
tightly closed and waiting for the
Bud Bunnies to open them.

Betsy could see the other
Bud Bunnies already setting to
work. As they twitched their noses

21

and each bud unfurled, beautiful
splashes of colour burst out. Betsy
couldn't wait to join in. She flew
over to the nearest stem and
placed her nose against its delicate

bud. Slowly, carefully, she got
ready to twitch her nose and . . .

'*Hic*!'

Betsy jumped backwards in
surprise, knocking the bud away.

'Oh, no!' she sighed. *Perhaps I need some more fresh air*, she thought. She took a deep breath. Then she carefully put her nose back to the flower.

'*Hic* – no!' she cried, as her nose jerked and bumped the bud away again. 'What am I going to – *hic* – do?'

The sound of laughter rang out across the meadow. Betsy turned to see where it was coming

from. There, on a grassy bank

behind her, was a little

Pollen Puppy. He was chuckling

so hard his golden wings were

jiggling up and down.

'You looked so funny,' he cried merrily. 'Do it again, do it again! Please!'

Betsy folded her paws and glared at him. Like all the fairy animals in Misty Wood, Pollen Puppies had an important job to do – spreading the golden pollen in the meadows and fields so the flowers could grow. But they were also very cheeky and loved to joke around.

'I'm not doing it on purpose, you know,' Betsy said. She felt quite cross. 'I've got the – *hic* – hiccups.'

'The hic-hiccups?' the puppy repeated, and burst out laughing again. 'Those are just the funniest hiccups I've ever seen.'

'Well, I don't think they're funny,' Betsy said. 'And neither will the rest of Misty Wood if I can't get these buds open and

looking pretty.' She slumped down in the long grass and began to cry.

The Pollen Puppy stopped laughing immediately. 'I'm very sorry,' he said quickly. 'I didn't mean to upset you.'

He scampered over to Betsy and patted her on the back. Although Pollen Puppies were mischievous, they were very kind fairy animals at heart.

'Look, don't cry,' he said.

'I think I know how you can get rid of your hiccups.'

'*Hic* – really?' Betsy gave a small sniff and wiped her eyes.

'*Hic* – really.' The puppy smiled. 'Follow me.'

CHAPTER THREE

Head Over Heels

'My name's Petey, by the way,' the puppy called back over his golden wings as they flew up into the warm air. 'What's yours?'

'Betsy,' she replied. She fluttered

her wings faster to keep up, but
it wasn't easy to fly when you
had the hiccups. Every time she
hiccupped she fell a bit behind.

Finally, they reached a
clearing. Down below them was a
huge pond. It glistened silver and
blue in the sunlight.

'Moonshine Pond!' exclaimed
Betsy, looking down. 'What are we
doing here?'

Petey guided her down gently

to the sandy shore of the pond. 'To get rid of hiccups you need to have a drink,' he explained.

'A drink?' Betsy shook her

head. 'Oh, no. It was drinking juice that *gave* me the hiccups. I don't think I ought to – *hic* – drink any more.'

Petey grinned. 'Ah, but you got the hiccups from drinking *forwards*,' he explained. 'So to get rid of them, you have to do the opposite. You have to drink *backwards*.'

Betsy was confused. 'Drink backwards? How am I supposed to drink backwards?'

Petey shrugged his shoulders.
'I'm not exactly sure,' he said.
'I heard my grandma say it to
my sister once when she had the
hiccups. It must have worked
because she hasn't had them since.
Come on!'

Betsy watched as Petey
dashed down to the edge of the
pond, where the pearly water
lapped over silver pebbles.

'It does look really nice,' Betsy

said, hopping after Petey. 'Perhaps it will do the – *hic* – trick.' She leaned forward to take a slurp of the sparkling water.

'No, not like that!' Petey cried.

Betsy froze. 'What's the – *hic* – matter?' she asked.

'You have to drink backwards, remember?' Petey said. 'Look, like this.'

He put his paws on her back and turned her round so that she

35

was facing away from the pond. 'Now,' he said. 'Lean backwards and take a drink.'

'Lean backwards?' Betsy shook her head. 'But that's – *hic* – impossible.'

'Do you want to get rid of your hiccups or not?' Petey asked.

Betsy gave a sigh and bent backwards until the tips of her ears dangled down into the water.

'Brrr. The water's cold!' she

squeaked. But then she hiccupped again. She leaned back even further so that the top of her head was in the water and her furry tummy was pointing up to the sky.

'Nearly there,' Petey called out cheerily. 'You'll soon have got rid of those – uh-oh – oh, no – oh, dear!'

SPL**ASH!**

Betsy had lost her balance. She tumbled head over heels

into the water and landed with a splishy sploshy PLOP,

right on her bottom.

'Ow ow ow!' she cried, clambering out of the pond. She shook the water from her whiskers and at the same time let out an enormous . . .

'HICCUP!'

Petey rolled about on the bank of Moonshine Pond, laughing and laughing.

'You looked so funny!' he gasped. 'Do it again! Please!'

'Stop – *hic* – saying that!'
Betsy thumped her furry white
foot. 'You said you would help me
get rid of my hiccups – *HIC* – but
now they're even – *HIC* – worse
than before. And I'm soaking wet!'

She stretched out her poor
bedraggled wings.

'Sorry,' Petey said again. 'But
it really wasn't my fault. Honestly,
Betsy, it can't be that hard to
drink backwards.'

'OK then,' Betsy said. 'If you think it's so easy, why don't you – *HIC* – try it?'

Petey clapped his front paws together and grinned. 'All right, little Bud Bunny. I'll show you how it's done.'

Petey marched down to the edge of the pond. Then he turned around and set his back legs wide apart. Slowly, he bent backwards, tipping his soft, furry head down

towards the water.

'See how easy it is?' he said.
'Look, I'm nearly there.'

But just at that moment his
legs began to wobble. 'Just a little
bit further,' he gasped. 'Whoa!'

There was an almighty

SPLASH

and this time it was
Petey who tumbled,
head over heels, into
the cold water.

Now it was Betsy's turn to laugh. 'You looked so funny!' she cried. 'Like a big golden frog hopping off a lily pad!'"

Petey bounded out of the pond, shaking his fur and sending water spraying in all directions.

'I suppose it serves me right,' he said with a chuckle. He flopped down on the grass beside

Betsy. 'Now we're both soaking. Drinking backwards isn't as easy as I thought.'

'No, it's not,' Betsy said, her smile fading. 'So, what am I going to do now?'

CHAPTER FOUR

The Best Cure for Hiccups Ever

Betsy and Petey stretched out on the bank. The sun felt lovely and warm on their damp fur and they soon began to dry out.

45

Betsy was still hiccupping though. 'Today has been the unluckiest day of my life,' she sighed. 'I've been looking forward to unfurling the flowers for a whole year, but at this rate I won't be able to open a single – *hic* – bud.'

Just at that moment, there was a rustle in the hedgerow behind them. A small black face with a pointy nose and tiny eyes peered

46

at them grumpily.

'Hey, what's going on out there?' the creature said to them crossly. 'All your noise woke me up with a start.'

'Oh, no, it's – *hic* – Marley,' Betsy whispered to Petey.

'*Hic* – who?' Petey whispered back.

'Marley the Moonbeam Mole,' Betsy explained. 'He's a – *hic* – friend of my mum and dad's.

We're in trouble now.'

Marley squeezed his velvety little body out of his hiding place. He shook out his glittery wings and made his way towards them.

'He doesn't look very happy,' Petey whispered.

'Of course he's not,' Betsy said. 'Moonbeam Moles sleep during the day because they – *hic* – have to work all night.'

'Of course,' Petey said. 'They catch the moonbeams to put in the pond to make it all shimmery.'

'Exactly.' Betsy nodded. 'So, right now, Marley should be fast asleep.'

49

'Betsy, is that you?' Marley's tiny eyes blinked blindly.

'Hello, Marley. Yes, it's me,' said Betsy.

The sleepy mole's velvety brow furrowed. 'What are you doing all the way over here? It's the first day of spring. Shouldn't you be busy in the meadow opening the buds?'

'She was,' Petey quickly explained. 'I was the one who brought her here. Sorry.'

50

'So you should be, young Pollen Puppy,' Marley grumbled. 'How am I supposed to sleep with all of your chatting and splashing going on?'

'We're so sorry, Marley,' Betsy said quickly. 'We didn't mean to – *hic* – wake you. *HIC*!'

'Goodness me,' Marley gasped. 'Those hiccups sound serious.'

'They are,' Betsy said glumly.

'I've had them all morning and I haven't been able to open a – *hic* – single flower.'

'I thought drinking backwards might cure them,' Petey added. 'So that's why we came to your pond.'

Marley shook his head and gave a little chuckle. 'I've heard of that old cure,' he said. 'I'm not sure it works every time. But don't worry, I have a much better idea.'

'You do?' Betsy and Petey cried.

52

'Yes, I do. Now listen carefully.'
Marley beckoned them closer with
his little pink paw. 'What I am about
to tell you is the best cure for hiccups
ever invented.'

'It is?' Betsy exclaimed. She and
Petey leaned in eagerly.

'To get rid of hiccups,'
Marley whispered, 'you need
to be surprised by something *so*
surprising that your hiccups forget
to hiccup.'

Betsy and Petey looked
at each other. 'Something *so*
surprising that your hiccups
forget to hiccup,' Betsy repeated.
'But I've already done so many
surprising things today, Marley.
Getting hiccups in the first place

was surprising. Meeting Petey
was surprising. And falling into
the water was definitely – *hic* –
surprising!'

Petey shook his golden head.
'Those things can't have been
surprising enough,' he said.

'Exactly.' Marley nodded.
'But I'm sure something will come
along that you really weren't
expecting.' Then he gave a big
yawn and stretched out his arms.

'I'm afraid I'm very sleepy. So if you don't mind, I will leave you to find the cure by yourselves. Good luck. And goodnight!'

'Good – *hic* – night,' Betsy said. 'And thank you, Marley – *hic*!'

As Betsy watched Marley shuffle off to his bed, Petey somersaulted past her, wagging his tail.

'What are you doing, Petey?'

Betsy laughed.

'Trying to surprise the hiccups out of you,' Petey said, standing up and catching his breath. 'Did it work?'

'I don't – *hic* – think so,' Betsy said.

'Hmm.' Petey scratched his head. With a sudden whoop and twirl, he flew up into the air and performed a series of loop-the-loops in the clear blue sky.

'Any good?' he called.

'*Hic* – no, sorry,' Betsy called back. 'But it is making me dizzy just looking at you.' She closed her eyes for a moment to get rid of the dizziness.

When she opened them again, Petey had completely disappeared. Betsy spun this way and that, trying to catch a glimpse of the little Pollen Puppy, but he was nowhere to be seen.

'Where – *hic* – are you?' Betsy called.

'Boo!' Petey cried, jumping out from behind a clump of clover.

Betsy let out a little squeal and fell backwards, landing on her fluffy tail. 'Petey, what are you doing?' she said.

'I'm still trying to surprise you.' Petey shook the leaves from his ears and bounded over to her. 'Is it working?'

'I don't – *hic* – think so, but thank you for trying so hard.' Betsy slumped to the ground in despair. 'I've tried fresh air and sunshine

and drinking backwards and being surprised. But nothing seems to work. I'm beginning to think I'll have these *hic*-hiccups for – *hic* – ever!'

CHAPTER FIVE

Gee Whiskers!

Betsy's silky ears flopped down over her face. She felt very miserable indeed.

'Don't give up,' Petey said, sitting down in front of her.

'Misty Wood is full of helpful fairy animals. Sooner or later we're bound to meet someone who *really* knows how to cure your hiccups.'

'Do you – *hic* – think so?' Betsy lifted her little pink nose and tried to smile.

'Yes, I do,' Petey replied firmly. 'Why don't we go a little further into the wood and see who we can find?'

'OK,' Betsy said, nodding her
soft white head. 'And while we
fly, I'm going to take lots of deep
breaths of fresh air.'

'Good plan,' Petey grinned.
'Come on, follow me!'

He flicked his wings and took
off into the sky, with Betsy close
behind. This time they swooped
low over Misty Wood, hoping to
catch a glimpse of someone else
who could help them.

As she flew over Heather Hill, Betsy breathed in the delicious scent of the purple heather. But that didn't cure her hiccups.

In Bluebell Glade they played chase with the butterflies. But that didn't cure her hiccups either.

As they flew, Betsy noticed the hard work her fellow Bud Bunnies had done. Lots of flowers had been opened, making Misty Wood look like a brightly coloured patchwork

quilt. How she wished she could join the other bunnies!

Next, they flew towards a sunny clearing. Even here there were hundreds of new buds just waiting to be opened.

'Please can we land? Betsy asked. She couldn't help wanting to take a closer peep. 'Oh, Petey,' she sighed as they landed in the springy grass. 'I should – *hic* – be unfurling these buds.'

67

'And you will be soon,' Petey said. 'I just know it.'

'I hope so,' Betsy said. 'Because I'm starting to get very tired and my wings have gone all

droopy. It's hard work having the hiccups, you know.'

Just then, the glinting sunlight on the grass faded and darkness fell over the clearing.

'Is it night-time already?' Betsy exclaimed.

'No,' Petey replied. 'It's a shadow. And it's coming from that huge creature over there.'

They both looked up to see a massive figure coming slowly

69

towards them through the woods. Its face was covered in darkness, but the shadow it cast was very big.

'Who do you think it is?' Petey whispered, grabbing Betsy by the paw.

'I don't know,' Betsy said. 'It's very big – maybe it's a giraffe.'

'But giraffes don't live in Misty Wood!' Petey pulled Betsy behind a bush.

'Who's there?' the big shadowy figure called in a deep voice.

'Maybe it's an elephant?' Betsy whispered.

Petey shook his head. 'Elephants don't live here either.'

'I said, who's there?' the voice boomed again.

Petey put his paw to his mouth, signalling to Betsy to keep quiet. Betsy nodded, but as she did so, she let out an enormous . . .

BETSY THE BUNNY

'HICCUP!'

GEE WHISKERS!

At once the footsteps began *thump thump thumping* towards the bush.

'I know someone's there,' the voice called again.

Petey and Betsy exchanged glances.

'I bet you two hazelnut buns it's a tiger!' Petey whispered.

THUD.

The footsteps came closer.

'With really big feet!' Petey hissed again.

THUMP.

The ground around them began to shake.

'And a really huge body!' Petey continued.

SWISH!
SWOOSH!

The bush began to rustle.

'And a really long tail,' Petey finished.

'But – *HIC* – tigers don't live here either!' Betsy gasped.

'Come out!' the voice boomed, very, very close now.

Betsy and Petey looked at each other.

Betsy took a deep breath, and forgetting about her hiccups, decided to be brave. 'I bet you two

hazelnut buns it *isn't* a tiger!' she said, and peeped out from behind the bush.

'Gee whiskers!' she cried in astonishment. 'I can't believe it's you!'

CHAPTER SIX

A Surprise so Surprising . . .

'Who is it? Who is it?' Petey

whispered from his hiding place.

But Betsy was so surprised

that she couldn't answer him.

'Is it a tiger with really big feet and a really huge body and a really long tail?' Petey asked.

'No!' Betsy cried in delight. 'It's – it's – the Easter Bunny!'

Petey came bounding out from behind the bush. 'The Easter Bunny?' he yapped excitedly. 'Are you sure?'

The fairy animal friends both rubbed their eyes with their paws and looked again. Sure enough,

towering over them was a very large white bunny. He had a bright pink nose, pointy ears and long, feathery whiskers. In his front paws he held a huge basket of brightly coloured eggs.

'Oh, Mister Easter Bunny, sir,' Betsy cried. 'I'm so pleased to meet you. You are my hero! You are my favourite bunny in the whole wide world – apart from my mum and dad and baby brother,

Bobby, of course. Oh, and my grandma and grandpa and great uncle Boris. And my cousin Bella.' Betsy grinned. 'But after all of them, you're my favourite bunny for sure! The eggs you bring are so delicious, and it's so much fun trying to find them.' She took a hop backwards and gazed up at the huge Easter Bunny. 'I can't believe I've met you. I always hoped, but I never dreamed I'd

actually be so
lucky!' Betsy
tilted her head
to one side. 'But
why are you
here? It's only the

first day of spring. Easter isn't for
ages. Oh, this is so exciting isn't
it, Petey?' Betsy turned to Petey
and clapped her paws.

Petey just kept on grinning.

'Well, you certainly are a

talkative little Bud Bunny,' the Easter Bunny said, smiling down at Betsy. 'But I'm afraid I can't stop for long because I am in the middle of a very important job.'

'Ooh, what is it?' Betsy cried.

The Easter Bunny bent right down so that he could whisper in her ear. 'The reason I am here, little Bud Bunny, is to *practise* hiding eggs for the Misty Wood Easter Egg Hunt.'

'Practise?' Betsy's eyes opened wide.

The Easter Bunny nodded. 'How do you think I get so good at hiding them?'

'That's just like me opening the flowers with my nose,' Betsy said. 'It takes a lot of practise to get it right.' She looked down at the floor and her fluffy white ears flopped down over her face. 'But I haven't got *any* right this year.'

The Easter Bunny put down
his basket of eggs. 'Why ever not?'
'Something awful has
happened,' Betsy said sadly.

'I've got the worst case of hiccups ever. Lots of fairy animals have tried to help me cure them, but nothing has worked. Petey and I were looking for someone else who might be able to help.'

'I think –' Petey began.

But Betsy hadn't finished. 'Mister Easter Bunny, sir, you've reminded me that the wood always looks so pretty when we have the Misty Wood Easter Egg Hunt.'

'I think –' Petey said again, but Betsy kept talking.

'But this year,' she said, sniffing miserably, 'it's not going to look *nearly* so pretty because I haven't been able to help unfurl all the buds. Oh dear, I don't –'

'Ssh!' The Easter Bunny held up a big paw and Betsy stopped talking at once.

'Do you realise,' the Easter Bunny said in his kindly voice,

88

'that you haven't hiccupped once since you've been talking to me? I think, my dear Bud Bunny, that your hiccups might finally be cured!'

'That's what I've been trying to say!' Petey said with a giggle.

Betsy clapped her paws with glee. 'You're right!' She paused and swallowed hard a few times. 'I don't feel hiccuppy at all.' She fluttered her pink wings and fluffed

up her whiskers. Then she turned to Petey. 'Marley the Moonbeam Mole was right after all. I *have* been surprised by something so surprising that my hiccups have forgotten to hiccup!'

CHAPTER SEVEN

Hic Hic Hooray!

Betsy was so happy that she did a little hop in the air, landing right at the Easter Bunny's feet. 'Thank you, thank you, thank you!' she cried. 'You are the best surprise *ever*!'

The Easter Bunny chuckled.

'I'm very glad to hear it,' he said.

Betsy did another bunny
hop. 'Oh, Easter Bunny. Is there
anything I can do to repay you
for curing my hiccups?'

The Easter Bunny smiled down at Betsy. 'Well,' he began, 'it just so happens that there *is* something you could do. Both of you, in fact.' He turned to look at Petey too.

'Oh, yes.' The little puppy wagged his tail eagerly. 'Anything at all.'

The Easter Bunny tweaked his whiskers thoughtfully. 'Well, as I told you, I'm here to do a very

93

important job – practising hiding the eggs for the Easter Egg Hunt.'

'Yes! Yes!' Petey said, chasing his tail with excitement.

'But how can I tell if I've hidden them really well, unless I have some helpers trying to find them?' the Easter Bunny said, his eyes twinkling.

A huge smile spread across Betsy's face. 'You mean, you'd like *us* to try and find them?'

The Easter Bunny nodded.

'If you would be so kind.'

'Gee whiskers! That is the best job ever!' Betsy exclaimed.

Petey rolled on to his back and waved his paws in the air with delight.

'So you'll do it?' the Easter Bunny said.

'Yes!' Betsy and Petey cried at the tops of their voices.

'Thank you,' the Easter

Bunny said warmly. 'Well, first of all, I need you to close your eyes while I hide two eggs. And no peeping!'

'We won't,' Betsy said. She closed her eyes tightly and listened to the rustling of leaves as the

Easter Bunny set about hiding the eggs.

'All right, you can open them now,' the Easter Bunny called.

'This is so much fun!' Petey said as they started flying about looking for the eggs.

Betsy looked under bushes and on top of branches.

Petey looked behind stones and inside nests.

The Easter Bunny leaned

against an oak tree and watched
as they searched high and low.
'It looks as if I have done a most
excellent job,' he said.

Betsy was just about to give
up when she caught a glimpse of
something shimmering behind a
lavender bush. Very carefully, she
reached a paw inside the bush
and pulled out a beautiful pink
speckled egg. 'It matches my
wings!' she beamed.

The Easter Bunny chuckled. 'So it does.'

Across the clearing, Petey pulled a chocolate egg from a hollow tree trunk and let out a cheer. 'I found one too!' he cried.

Betsy and Petey flew over to the Easter Bunny with their eggs.

'Well done,' he said, smiling down at them.

'I didn't think we were ever going to find them,' Betsy said.

'So you don't think I need any more practice at hiding them?' the Easter Bunny said.

Betsy shook her head. 'No! You're the world's best hider ever.'

She went to put the beautiful pink egg back in his basket, but the Easter Bunny put a fluffy white paw out. 'You can keep it,' he said. 'After all, it does match your wings.'

'Can I keep mine?' Petey asked, looking longingly at the chocolate egg. 'It matches my paws ... sort of.'

The Easter Bunny nodded.
'In that case, you must.'

Betsy licked the pink egg. It tasted delicious, like spun sugar.

Petey took a bite from his chocolate egg. 'Yum!' he said, licking his lips.

The Easter Bunny watched, smiling as they gobbled up their eggs. 'Well, now I must be off,' he said when they'd finished.

'Already?' Betsy said.

The Easter Bunny picked up his basket. 'I'm afraid so. But don't forget, you have something else to do now your hiccups have gone,' he grinned as he waved goodbye.

Betsy put her paw to her mouth. 'My buds!' she cried.

'Come on, Petey, we need to get going. Goodbye, Mister Easter Bunny, sir, and thank you!'

With a last wave, the Easter Bunny hopped off into Misty Wood

103

and Betsy and Petey took to the sky once more. They flew swiftly to Honeydew Meadow, where Betsy's buds were still waiting to be opened.

'Here goes,' Betsy muttered as she landed next to an unfurled flower. 'Wish me luck, Petey.'

'Good luck, Betsy,' whispered Petey.

Cautiously, Betsy shuffled up to the nearest flower.

Very slowly, she put her tiny
pink nose to the tightly furled bud.

She waited for just a moment.
Had her hiccups really gone?
Would she be able to keep still for
long enough?

She placed her nose gently
against the delicate petals,
and twitched. At first, nothing
happened. Then, slowly, the petals
started to unfurl. Betsy gasped as
the flower burst into life.

105

Each petal was as soft as satin and as bright as a jewel. She had never seen anything quite so pretty.

'I did it, I did it!' squeaked Betsy, hopping back to admire her handiwork.

Petey cheered and clapped. 'I knew you could,' he cried, 'once you got rid of those hiccups.'

'Well, I'm very glad they've gone, Petey,' she said. 'But I'm also very glad I had them.'

HIC HIC HOORAY!

'Really? But why?' Petey said.

Betsy beamed at him.

'Because if I hadn't got the hiccups, I would never have met you. And you would never have agreed to help me. And we would never have gone all over Misty Wood searching for a cure. And we would never have found the Easter Bunny.

'So, you see, I made a new friend *and* got to meet my hero all

in one day. And all because of the hiccups!'

Petey did a little flip of joy. 'In that case, I say three cheers for hiccups!'

'I agree!' Betsy cried. 'Hic hic, hooray!'

Turn the page for lots of fun Misty Wood activities!

Join the dots

Follow the numbers and join up all the dots to make a lovely picture from the story.

Start with dot number 1. When you've finished joining all the dots, you can colour the picture in!

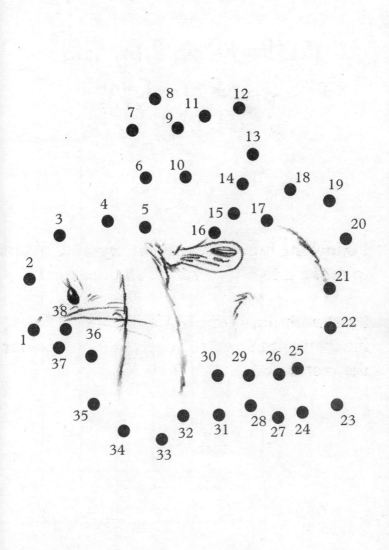

Help Betsy and Petey find their Easter Eggs!

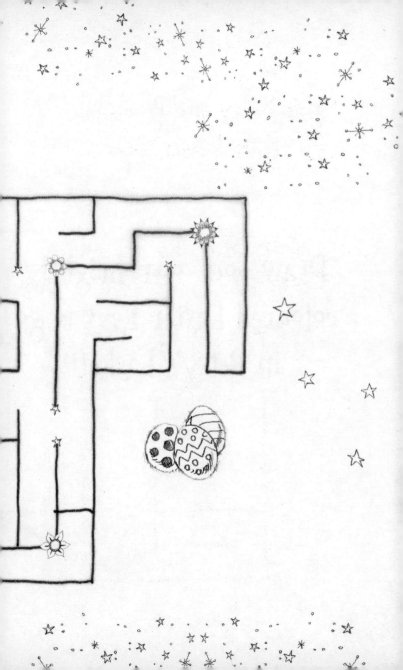

Draw your own brightly coloured Easter Eggs to go in Betsy's basket!

Fairy Animals
of Misty Wood

Meet all the fairy animal friends!

Look out for
Daisy the Deer
and lots more
coming soon . . .

Meet the

Fairy Animals
of Misty Wood

There's a whole world to explore!

Download the FREE *Fairy Animals* app and visit **fairyanimals.com** for lots of gorgeous goodies . . .

- ✳ Free stuff
- ✳ Games
- ✳ Write to your favourite characters
- ✳ Step inside Misty Wood
- ✳ Send us your cute pet pictures
- ✳ Make your own fairy wings!